I0530988

THAT HOUSE ON DAKOTA STREET:

A JO DANNING SHORT STORY

RAE T. ALEXANDER

Copyright Beary and Blevins Publishing, 2016

All Rights Reserved.
This is a work of fiction and the city of Taylor or any other
fictional character does not represent any living person or
organization.

TABLE OF CONTENTS

1

Chapter 1

The house on that rugged street was not ordinary. The faded colors of green, purple, and orange surrounded the house with their uneven horizontal stripes. Windows coated with unidentifiable and sticky debris and dead bugs offered no view for the curious. Unattended grass and weeds crept upward against the brick base of the house, while overloaded garbage cans provided decoration for one side of the mysterious house with their glitter of silver and their patches of rust.

The yard was empty of the type of green grass that many of the other yards in the neighborhood possessed.. The street was located in a proud city of the South, in the state of North Carolina. Large yards were typical. Backyards were for barbeques, parties, and for the riding of the lawn mowers by the zealous and proud males of the household.

The house was odd in other ways as well. Its occupants were unemployed, unschooled, and mentally challenged by any interaction with what most people called, "life." People in the neighborhood generally avoided the house and the people living inside it.

"Don't go near those retards, Jo!" my grandmother said to me. While she spoke, she shook her glass of ice tea to chill it down.

I sat in a lounge chair beside her with whirling curiosity and judgmental eyes, but I kept my thoughts to myself with a guarded tongue. There was no need to chide my grandmother for being old-fashioned or politically incorrect. She was old and from another era. She spoke her bigotry so elegantly and properly that no one could ever accuse her of anything else but ignorance.

I was a visitor. I had just retired from the Air Force as a linguist. I had left the military and a husband. I was weighing my options for the next chapter of my life. My son, Casey, my thirteen- year-old, born on a military base in the United Kingdom, was with me but annoyed.

"Mama, I want to watch television," he said.

"Fine. Go inside," I gave in, and I motioned Casey away. Then my grandmother dropped her surprise.

"I'm leaving you the house, Jo, you and Casey" she said. "You were always my favorite."

It was true. My grandmother and I had a special relationship. We had spent many hours—when I was growing up—laughing at ridiculous jokes late into the night, to the point of annoying my grandfather. After he passed away, the jokes did not seem to be as funny. Laughter requires some awkward attention, I suppose.

I looked at my grandmother's odd attire. She wore a plain dress—a working dress, she called it—and black, rubber, knee-high boots. Her dress had a pattern of brown flowers against a dark brown and yellow background. It helped to camouflage the occasional red mud that splashed on it when my grandmother hoed the garden. Neither the dress nor the mud was quite complimentary.

"You don't have to do that, grandmother," I said. "I may not even live here. You know how I like the coast better."

I always did prefer the water. I loved watching the waves roll in from the horizon. A piedmont region, away from the coast, was simply a bore. It was all so defined, but the water was boundless—an escape—freedom.

I was taking a week off before I drove to Wilmington to shop for houses. My divorce settlement would provide a decent place to live, along with some savings that I had managed to put aside, money not seen by a cheating husband that had other things to monitor and control.

I looked forward to a new career in Wilmington also. A reporter friend of mine had invited me to meet her manager. I had just finished my degree in journalism, and I was anxious to find both a new home and a new job. Although it was nice to reminisce about the good old days with my grandmother, I was itching to leave and start my next adventure in life.

However, the one thing that I had always been curious about was that house that was beside my grandmother's garden. I often thought of it when I was growing up. My friends at school would tease me about living next to "those people" just before I would take a seat on the school bus.

Grandmother's house was once home to my mom and me when I was in high school. I was educated from an early age in the ways of a broken home. Most of my friends had the advantages of having both a mother and a father. I used to comfort my mind and make believe that my father was on a secret mission for the government. My friends never teased me about having one parent, but I felt embarrassed and vowed never to place my future children in that environment. Promises were made to be broken.

Imagination was often used in my childhood to bring to me whatever I was missing. I filled any gaps of the unexplained or the misunderstood with inventions or explanations that made sense to me. I had done so with my father who had abandoned my mother to marry a preacher's daughter, after their affair had split a church in half. My invention of him being on a secret mission with the CIA was a much better memory. Memories were manipulated by my inventive and creative imagination.

That house on Dakota Street was no exception. I imagined several stories to justify its peculiarity. I invented aliens that came down and performed experiments inside that left its occupants deformed and without brain control. I invented a family of cannibals that hunted at night for unwilling participants in various rituals of evil.

The oddness of the family within was sometimes displayed openly. The first occupant that I remember was a tall and skinny old man with short grey hair. He usually paraded in nothing but overalls and military combat boots. He usually walked around the backyard as if he was supervising the growth of the dead grass that covered most of the lot.

The supposed wife of the man usually did not leave the house. It was an extremely rare sight. She wore a long black wig. I often imagined a bald head underneath with many bumps and signs of horrible diseases. When she did show herself, she was always shouting orders and pointing at things. Perhaps, I thought, she was in charge of where to bury the bodies in the backyard. Perhaps, she occasionally saw a protruding finger that wiggled in the ground. The only words that I ever distinctly heard her say were, "I got to pee!" That sentence led to her hobbling around and taking her short body quickly to the back door at her fastest sprint.

They had two children. When I say children, I only speak of the relationship. The children were grown men. The town knew their names because they hired them for jobs that the spoiled white kids did not want to do. They cleaned up mobile home lots that had leaves and trash on it that had decayed through the winter. They moved heavy items into trucks, like broken refrigerators or washing machines. They performed manual labor for cash payment. Sometimes they kept some of the items in their backyard. They hoarded them for a future sale. Entrepreneurship knew no educational level. Their names were Bill and Tony.

Bill never said anything, to any person, at any time. He just nodded, I remember. Tony, on the other hand, had many things to say—and quite frequently. He had several popular sentences, but my favorite was when he said to me, mispronouncing my name, "Hi Joey, you bitch!" He would use other words that he had picked up from the local teenagers, but he often cussed me out while he smiled at me. He was a friendly guy that swore. He gave many people the middle finger as he laughed at them. He rode his bike throughout the neighborhood, and sometimes he saw me at my house just before I got on the school bus. Those were my memories of the two "boys."

I remember that there were some kind souls that had once attempted to rehabilitate the family. They took them to church with great hopes of turning them into Christians. They were concerned about their eternal souls, they claimed. Although, I questioned the logic. If salvation required a conscious and intellectual decision, I thought, how was that going to be possible with these people.

"Grandmother?"—I came out of my musings and asked my grandmother a question that had troubled me. "Are all of the family members over there still alive?"

"I haven't seen any of them in a few months. I don't actually know," she said, as she suddenly turned on me with a rare scolding. "Don't you go getting any ideas either. Those people are nothing but trash—and they smell."

She was right about the smell. Every time that one of them got remotely close to me, I would often be overwhelmed by the stench that spoke of weeks of neglect. The old woman smacked her toothless gums, just like the old man. Bill's teeth were a golden yellow when he smiled, and Tony's were a crooked brown and black. Hygiene was a foreign concept in that house on Dakota Street.

That House on Dakota Street

The biggest day of the month for the family, as I remembered it, was their monthly trip to "town." The entire family would hitch a ride every first week of the month, usually by a miserly employer that counted the trip as part of one of the boy's wages. The big trip was to the bank—to cash their social benefits check, a check that pissed off many locals that frowned upon the leeches that stole their tax money. People that lived on the government were nothing but scum, according to many in the community. There was a strong belief in the motto: "If one doesn't work, then they should not eat." At the same time, they ignored the sin of their own gluttony and hypocrisy, while they selectively pronounced their judgement on the unfortunate or the disadvantaged poor.

I looked back at the house after drinking my last bit of tea. It was then that I saw something that made me cuss in front my religious grandmother. I had not meant to use the "F" word. It just slipped out.

"Jo!" my grandmother yelled at me.

"Not now," I said, as I got up from the chair and marched away. My little boy, my precious little boy, Casey, was playing in the yard—in the yard of that distasteful house. Television had not been enough amusement for him.

I ran through the mucky garden without regard to the red mud. I yelled out Casey's name as I saw him digging up something in the dirt.

"**L**ook mama!" my excited adventurer exclaimed, as I prepared to yank an arm up. "A treasure box!"

My son had inherited his vivid imagination from me. Casey had found nothing but a shiny tobacco tin. Its lettering was faded, and his hand had reached inside just before we both heard the back door of the house unlock.

"Leave it!" I ordered him. "Let's get back to the house. Come on!"

He threw the box back to the yard, after I saw him quickly pocket something. We both trudged through the garden before realizing that there was another way. We stepped out of the garden and took the slow path around on the wet but mud-free pathway filled with Johnsongrass.

My son had named it Johnsongrass. That was how I knew its name. My son's hobby was botany. Besides his curious nature, he had also inherited my intelligence, although not my interests. He had been pronounced "gay" by his friends that preferred video games and movies. My child was only truly fascinated by plants.

I led him back inside grandmother's house while I gave her some assurance that everything was fine.

"He's ok, Grandmother," I said as I passed her. She just shook her iced tea and went back to staring at her garden.

Once inside and back in my son's bedroom, I started my official inquiry.

"What did you take out of the box?" I queried.

He pulled out the contents and placed them on a desk in the room. It was a piece of paper wadded up and two coins. I carefully unfolded the paper, as I detected that it was old and delicate. It had bold lettering on it and read, "State of North Carolina." It also had on the left side of it the words, "ten cents."

Chapter 2

"Confederate money, son," I told him. "Don't spend it all at once."

Then my eyes fell on the two coins that were on the desk. They were five dollar gold coins that had the word "Bechtler" on them. My husband had once collected old coins, and I had seen those kind before in a magazine. These were worth a lot of money, if they were not fake, I thought.

"We have to give these back, son," I spoke, but I realized the meaning of what I had just said. I would have to interact with these people, or at least someone would. I thought of calling the police, but soon kicked that idea out of my head. My son had been a thief. It would be better if I handled this myself.

"But I found it," Casey insisted. "It was buried. They didn't want it."

I gave my reasons and explained the ideas of private property to my botanist. Then I led him outside on a trek back to the house. My grandmother had started to pull weeds in her bean patch. At least I would not have to give an explanation to her, I thought. I could avoid that discussion for later.

I decided that my son and I would take the long way around. We walked on the side of the road in front of the house and past several houses on our way to Dakota Street. It was like a journey through history.

We past an old couple that was sitting on their porch swing. They both waved their nosey hands at us, as they mumbled something. In this neighborhood, the residents usually went out of their way to look at any stranger or unusual sight that passed by. Everyone knew everyone's business, or at least invented it.

The rest of the neighbors were gone. It was Thursday, a work day for most people. Many of the people on this street were employed by a magnet factory nearby, or the local mall. Service jobs were the primary industry in town. Although many of the folks commuted daily to Charlotte for office or computer jobs. There were two call centers also, but they were about an hour away. If you could commute, then you could have decent wages. However, your gas and automobile repair bill would eat up your salary.

The city of Taylor, North Carolina had a long and interesting history of development. It had been the home of a Civil War prison. It had been the center of a great Methodist revival where the evils of gambling and drinking had been yelled out to vast crowds of sinners. It had been the city of great debate and controversy when the local high school argued the merits for the use of the name "rebel" for its proud football team.

The city was known for its disparity of income and educational and cultural levels. Downtown Taylor had its antebellum houses in the historic district that housed usually no one at all. The city had a symphony orchestra that played about five concerts per year. There were two private colleges that were overpriced, but they provided a liberal education in the middle of a conservative population that had barely completed high school. The schools were started by wealthy heirs of a tobacco plantation.

Minimum wage was the dominant salary, and the local newspaper often had exuberant ads that proclaimed the benefit and advantage of positions that only promised a salary that was far below the poverty level.

It was no wonder that I often received the treatment of being someone who thought that they were better than everyone else. Even though I had been raised in Taylor, I was an outsider after I had left for college and the military. I had broken the rules. I had learned things. I was no longer one of "them."

Once my son and I arrived at the oddly colored house, we

both swallowed a gulp of preparation and attended to our objective. I rapped twice on the door and noticed the peeling paint on the wood. There was no response, so I knocked again with more force. Vines had grown up the sides of the door and tall weeds had surrounded the concrete steps. This side of the house was the view that could not be seen from my grandmother's garden. This side was shaded by trees and was much cooler.

We both heard the sounds of the woman inside. She was cussing and ordering people around. We had caused a problem. The door eventually opened and the old man leaned out. He had glasses on. It was the first time that I had seen him with glasses. He could read? I found that even *I* was not immune to prejudice or hasty generalization.

"Shut up!" he turned and yelled back, silencing the mumblings of the woman. "What do you want?" It was directed so forcefully that I had to take a moment and remember why we were there.

"My son found something, by mistake," I apologized. I ordered Casey to give the money back to the man, but we both were yelled at and shrunk from his response.

"That ain't mine," he said. "Go on! Get the hell out of here!" He then used a few words that I was not glad to hear in front of my son. After those words, he continued, as he slammed the door. "Son of a bitch! Shut the hell up!"

We left the family fight and decided to take the long way back. The garden was the quickest way, but my grandmother was still working in it. The last thing that I needed was more fighting from my grandmother. I knew, if given a chance, she would persist with nosey questions about what we were doing.

As we walked away, my son grinned his victory to me.

"It's mine now," he said. "Isn't it?"

"I suppose," I admitted. "But those coins are worth a lot of money, if they are real."

"I'm rich!" he said proudly as we walked. "That patch of green grass was lucky!"

The words sounded eerie to me. I imagined a single patch of green grass sitting on top of a dead body that was slowly rotting away. My mind went back to my own nightmares about the house. It was a house that was popular during Halloween. I remembered when dozens of children fulfilled the dare to go knocking on its dark porch. I never participated, but I had heard many stories of monsters eating children and carrying axes.

"A patch of green grass?" I asked him.

"Yeah. Everything around it was dead except the green circle of grass. It smelled weird also," Casey said.

We walked back and arrived at the back porch, and then we were greeted by my grandmother who was using a hose to wash off her boots.

"Suppertime coming up," she said. "Go inside and wash up. The casserole is almost ready."

My grandmother was a huge fan of making everything in one dish. Chicken casserole was one of her staples. She mixed chicken and sour cream like no one else could. Her kitchen produced amazing Southern dishes—although visitors often brought their own condiments to family reunions, as there were often one or two expired bottles of salad dressing in her refrigerator.

My grandmother was a frugal soul. She saved her ripped pantyhose with just a couple of strokes of clear fingernail polish. She washed and folded pieces of tin foil and placed them in drawers to use again and again. Her phrase of "eat it and name it" literally scared me to death. I always took a moment to insure fresh ingredients were used, and I usually turned down leftover food. She often kept frozen pork sandwiches in her freezer for months before thawing them out and eating them. The refrigerator was a box full of mystery.

Her fresh chicken casseroles were usually safe, and incredibly delicious. The smell was delightful as we entered the kitchen. The kitchen was the first room that one encountered from the carport. The front door that faced the main road was never used. It was appropriate to walk through the kitchen before any other room because it gave any visitor the feeling of home immediately.

"Go wash your hands," I told Casey as I peeked through the oven. I went to the kitchen sink to wash my hands while Casey went to the rear bathroom. As I washed my hands with dish soap, I looked out of the kitchen window above the sink. I saw the house and the old man in the yard in the distance, just beyond the garden

The old man was digging up the area where my son had taken the box. He had a wheelbarrow and two sacks in it. Again, my mind spun a tale to amuse. I imagined the man digging up a body and then relocating it somewhere else. He had been found out. He was covering his tracks, I thought.

"None of my business," I mumbled. "Weirdo."

My son came back and asked me what I was looking at. I told him that I was admiring the garden. The kitchen screen door was closed, but the other door was open. Casey pressed his face against the screen door with an attitude of boredom and impatience.

"When is dinner ready?" he asked. My son called it dinner, but my grandmother had always called it supper. A language was dying, I thought. Then I heard a question that sent me into a panic.

That House on Dakota Street

"What is grandmother doing laying on the steps like that?" he asked.

I rushed to the door and pushed him aside, and I went down the stairs to my collapsed grandmother.

She was dead.

3

That House on Dakota Street

"What are you going to do with the house, Jo?" he asked me. It was Tommy Ledbetter's way of eventually asking me out. He and several other mourners filled the house. The funeral had just concluded a few hours before.

Tommy had been an admirer for years, but I had left his attempted clutches for another life. Throughout high school, he had tried to court me, but with no success.

"Are you still married," I asked him, avoiding the question. He adjusted his tie against his sweaty white shirt that stuck to his heavy belly.

"Sue Ann and I got divorced two years ago. I'm a free man," he said, as he nudged me with a flirtatious elbow.

"Got a job for you, down at the paper," he said and winked.

Tommy had finished high school and had taken a management course through the mail that had certified him as a business professional. In truth, he had inherited the local paper through no merits of his own, except for being the only male child. The newspaper was managed by a corporation, but he was technically in charge of it. It was a fact that he often reminded people of when he was trying to impress them.

"Fact is—somebody just left—Trudy Jones, the columnist?" he said. "But I could give you the job—that is if you plan on staying around."

"I don't think so, Tommy," I told him. "I am going to Wilmington as soon as I secure a realtor for this place."

Tommy went to the kitchen sink and looked at the view of the garden and the mysterious house just beyond.

"Your grandmother was quite a woman. What happened to your folks?" he asked.

"My dad went off to Florida with his *woman*. We lost touch with him. My mom passed away in California two years ago," I told him. "My grandmother outsmarted and outlived them all, I guess."

"I see the Johnson family outlived everyone as well," he said as he pointed out the window.

It was the first time that I had actually heard the last name of the family that lived in that weird house. I was curious, but I knew it would cost me to find out more.

"Johnson family, huh? What is their story?" I asked him. Tommy was not only a newspaperman, but he was also one of the most annoying history buffs that I had ever known. He knew it all, even when he did not.

"That family has a ton of history," he said as he turned to me. "Why don't I tell you about it sometime—over dinner?"

My son interrupted the awkward moment, just in time.

"Mama, can I go outside and play?" he asked me. I sent him outside, but I insisted that he stay in the carport area. He left and took his remote control car, and I realized that I had sent him outside while he still wore his Sunday clothes. The crowd of mostly strangers and Tommy were getting on my last nerve.

"Cute kid," Tommy said. Tommy was also beginning to bore me, but my curiosity had to be satisfied.

"Why don't we go out to the garden, and you can tell me more about the Johnson family?" I insisted. Tommy frowned, but he accepted the bargain. At his age, and in his shape, his options were limited.

We walked the edges of the garden, and we stepped over the occasional stone and dog poop, a gift from a neighborhood mammal. His story began with his usual historical approach.

"That land over there used to be a "Freed" school," he said.

That House on Dakota Street

"A *what*?" I asked.

"A "Freed" school. It was a school house for African-American students," he said.

Knowing Tommy, I concluded that he had used that description rather than his usual racist term that I knew that he was more acquainted with. He was trying to impress me again, but I knew that he was not the liberal or open-minded person that he pretended to be.

"It used to be the home of Jeremiah Tucker, a sympathizer during the Civil War. He hid slaves in a cellar—way down deep in the ground, underneath that house," he said. "In fact, I believe that it stretched over into your grandmother's garden. He was shot, and the original house was burned and abandoned. That house has been there since about the 1930's. I think some old couple used to live there—I believe. Then around the sixties or seventies, this family showed up to the courthouse one day. They had papers that said that they owned it. Nobody wanted it, and they never questioned whether it was legal or not. The Johnson family has been there ever since."

"What happened to the couple that built the second house?" I asked him.

"Oh, you have to go to dinner to find that out, baby doll," he teased.

"Never mind," I said. I realized that he did not know anything else. If he had, he would have blabbed it all. It was in his nature.

"Just teasing—jeez," he admitted. "I don't know what happened. That's all I know."

The thought of an old cellar underneath a house intrigued me for a few minutes, but Wilmington and the coast were calling me. I had better things to do than look for historical relics.

Chapter 3

After the crowds and Tommy left, my son and I sat in the kitchen and munched on cookies and talked about our escape.

"Is Wilmington more exciting than Taylor?" he inquired.

"I suppose," I said. "You are going to love the ocean. It gives you strength and character."

"Whatever," he said, as he stuffed his mouth and followed it with a gulp of milk.

I then asked him what the large box was that he had out earlier. Just before the funeral, he was in the basement and had found a large box that he had taken to his room.

"It's broken. It doesn't have batteries anyway," he talked while his mouth was full.

Casey had found an explorer tool in the basement. It was a metal detector. It was plastic and cheap, but it was technically a metal detector. I had Casey show it to me after our snack. He was eager to try it out and see if it worked. His persistence forced me to take a trip to the local store for batteries, just to satisfy his mind. I knew that I would not get any sleep unless I complied.

When I returned, we found that it did, in fact, function as a metal detector. We spread out some quilts in the living room and tested it. It beeped when it detected our hidden forks and spoons. Curiosity had been satisfied.

"Now— can we get some sleep?" I asked him. "The realtor will be here first thing in the morning, and I need some rest. You can be a pirate tomorrow."

"Yes!" he said with excitement.

I tucked him in and realized how quiet the air was. The town of Taylor was quiet in general, but the inside of a house of a woman that had just passed away was just too peaceful—it was a peace that was quite disturbing. Sometimes quiet can drive one insane.

That House on Dakota Street

I decided that some gentle music was in order, so I looked for a radio in my grandmother's bedroom to mellow my fears. I needed a little bit of noise to calm my nerves before the sandman could visit me.

There was a radio near my grandmother's sewing machine and next to a window. It had no timer on it, but it was functional. I turned the knob and found a classical music station, and then I found a station that played light jazz, from one of the colleges in town. It was tranquil enough, so I left it on that one—but then I nearly screamed at what happened next.

The light near the radio had bounced on the window and had initially prevented me from seeing outside. When I reached for the table lamp, I could see past the reflection of the light. I saw a figure that stared at me with pronounced and frightening attention and raised eyebrows. It was the old man, from the Johnson place. He was outside the bedroom window and looking straight at me.

That House on Dakota Street

"Maybe you just dreamed it," my son said to me at breakfast. I was leery of partaking of the cereal initially. It took me about a minute to find the expiration date. Fortunately, it was still good, and we were able to have some breakfast. It was a plain cereal of oats, but my son knew where the sugar was. Little boys have ways of knowing those things, even in a strange house.

"I did not dream it," I said. "The old man was outside the window. I must have screamed loudly for you to wake up like you did."

Casey told me that when he had arrived there was no man outside. It was my son that had tucked *me* into bed, instead of the other way around. I awoke several times in a heavy sweat. It had been a while since I had experienced the warm Southern nights, especially in a house with no air conditioner. My grandmother had been a cold-natured person, and she saw no need for the expense of a machine that she would never use.

After breakfast, the realtor came and discussed with me the details of the property management and eventual sale. Casey took his metal detector outside and explored the garden.

"Cute kid," the older female realtor said. I could not help but think of Tommy when she said it. Do people have a limited vocabulary in this town, I thought.

"We may have a slight problem with the house," she told me.

It seemed that my grandmother had not told me about a few details about this gift of hers. There were taxes that had not been paid, and there was a lien against the house of over ten thousand dollars. The creditors were asking for their money.

"Can't I just refuse the house?" I asked her.

Chapter 4

"You need to talk to an attorney," she said. "Gabe Williams is good. I can get you in touch with him, if you want."

I sighed and thought of the additional delay. I imagined myself being swallowed up in Taylor—with Tommy asking me out on a daily basis. I was never going to get out of this place, I thought. I took down Gabe's number, and I walked the lady back to her car.

My son waved at me when he saw me. He was excited about his treasure hunt. Once the realtor drove away, I walked out to meet my adventurer.

"Mama, I found another coin!" he said and smiled. He pulled out another rare coin from his pocket and wiped it off.

The thought came to me about selling the coins and paying off the tax and liens on the place. Perhaps they were worth more than I could imagine, I thought.

"Casey," I said, as I looked at the piece of metal. "These coins are worth a lot of money and…"

"You can have them, mama," he volunteered. "If you need the money, you can have them."

I grabbed and hugged Casey. I held back my tears, but I felt so proud of my unselfish boy. He had not learned the bad habits of his father.

"Thank you, Casey," I said. "You go find as many as you can, and I am going to town and see how much money we can get."

I called Gabe Williams and made an afternoon appointment, and then I phoned a few friends and inquired about a pawn shop. I used the excuse about pawning some old watches that my grandmother had. I certainly did not want anyone to find out about my son's discoveries. My friends did not frequent pawn shops, so I looked in the telephone directory and picked one at random. The telephone directory was old, but I assumed that pawn shops were forever and did not close.

I found a pawn shop in the southwest part of Taylor, in an area that was not known for its safety. I drove the narrow streets to the shop, and I parked in a gravel parking lot. I found the owner inside along with several customers that had a bad smell to them. I whispered to the old gentleman owner that I wanted to speak to him in private about an item, and he escorted me to a back room.

"Most people like you don't come into a place like this," the African-American male said to me. "What you got?"

I opened my purse and took out an envelope. I removed the coins and handed them to him.

"Hmm," he said. "You the lady next to the Johnson place?" He was on to me, in a split second. He scratched his white hair and waited for my reaction.

"Yes," I admitted.

"You think I'm dumb or something? You don't like or trust black people?" he accused.

"Look, I just want to know how much these are worth," I said. I knew that I showed myself as being uncomfortable, but it had nothing to do with his race. I wanted to tell him that I was learned and accomplished. I was a college graduate and not a racist. I was educated and above this place, I thought. I imagined that he would not believe me, so I did not start into the rant.

"Above five thousand dollars, give or take a thousand or two," he said and handed them back to me. "Per piece, of course. You might even get up to ten thousand, if they are legitimate"

"Don't you know if they are?" I asked.

"They need to be tested, by an expert," he said, then he smiled at me. "You ain't from around here, are you?"

I told him that I had been gone for a long time and had been living abroad.

"I apologize for my insinuations earlier," the old gentleman said.

"What do you know about the Johnson place?" I asked him. I gave him a friendly smile.

"I know it's an old place, with a lot of history," he said. "That land used to belong to the indigenous people—long before the white man ever took it."

I showed an impressed face, and the man took it a step further.

"Yeah, lady. I went to college too. Surprised?" he asked.

I had been caught in a bit of racism and assumption. I was ashamed of it.

"Don't worry about it. You ain't like the rest of the people here," he said. "Take my advice. Get out of this city, as soon as you can."

I then further surprised the man and invited him to supper, later at my grandmother's house. He then surprised me and accepted. He promised to shed some light on some history later that night.

I left the pawn shop with a renewed sense of trust in humanity, and then I made a brief stop at the attorney's office. Gabe Williams was in and insisted on meeting me even though I was early. He turned on his best Southern charm.

"Ms. Danning, come on in," Gabe said. He dismissed his secretary and escorted me into his office. "I hear you have all kinds of problems with that house of yours."

"There seems to be some money owed, yes," I said as I took a seat. The entire office was an antique. Everything was plush and spoke of either age or dignity. The chair was uncomfortable, but it looked expensive. It was glossy and firm, like most everything else in the room.

"Let me see, now," he said, as he looked through an open file on his desk. "Jocelyn Danning—and your grandmother's name was Peck?" I then confirmed with a nod. I was annoyed by his delay and slowness. Perhaps, I was prejudiced against all people. In my travels, perhaps, I had become a snob.

"I hear you want to disclaim the property? Is that correct?" he asked.

"Yes. Is there a problem?" I asked.

"Only slightly. Your grandmother willed the house to Casey, not you," he said.

5

That House on Dakota Street

I was the guardian of my son, and my son owned a house with a garden full of treasure. It seemed like Taylor was in control of my life. Wilmington would have to wait. I had legal issues to attend to.

That night at supper, my son watched television while Mr. Jennings and I discussed the Johnson place in the kitchen. He even helped with the dishes. We drank coffee and began our discussion.

"I left and graduated from Howard, believe it or not," he said. "I came back and took over my dad's pawn shop. I thought that I would be gone in a few months. But life and three kids later…"

"Your wife passed away?" I asked.

"She died a few years ago. Cancer," he said. "God has a cruel sense of humor. I wanted to go to New York, but love said otherwise."

"It ain't all about God. People make choices, and fall or die by them," I said.

"You don't believe in God?" he asked.

"I ain't sure what I believe in these days, Mr. Jennings—certainly not fate," I said.

Mr. Jennings began his story about the Johnson place. He said it was a cursed piece of land.

"That is why nobody wanted it," he said. "The Native Americans that originally owned that piece of land were Cherokee. They were driven off this land, by a family by the name of Tucker."

I recalled Tommy's words to me about a Jeremiah Tucker during the Civil War. Mr. Jennings told me that a revival had come to town and had frightened poor Mr. Tucker into salvation.

"He felt guilty about what his family did to the Cherokee people," he said. "He became religious, and a sympathizer.

Chapter 5

"He helped the slaves avoid persecution. He hid them and then secretly helped them to escape. You see, Ms. Danning—sometimes, even the most evil people in the world can become good people. Devils can become saints, or even angels. There is good in everybody. Don't ever forget that."

I thanked him for the sermon, and then we said our goodbyes. He knew little else about the Johnson family. He assumed like everyone else that they were drifters that had just taken advantage of a situation and had just moved into the house with forged papers. He left with a word of advice.

"You may want to stay and dig around a bit," he said. "You might find some treasure underneath your plants out there. You never know. If I were you, I would dig about a six-foot hole, right in the middle of the garden."

I walked Mr. Jennings down the back steps and to his car. He drove away, and then I went back inside to check on my son. He had fallen asleep on the couch.

I turned off the television and secured a blanket from the closet. I covered Casey and then retired to my bedroom. I looked briefly at the radio, but I was too scared to turn it on. I certainly did not want another visitor to greet me again at the window.

I took out my cell phone in the hopes of playing a game, and then lay on the bed and relaxed. The cell phone coverage was horrible in Taylor, but my downloaded game worked just fine.

"Mama!"—I heard my son scream. I jumped up and ran to the living room. I then remembered that I had forgotten to lock the back door. It was the Johnson man, and he stood by my son. He held an axe to his throat, and spoke his demands. He smelled profusely and wore only his overalls and combat boots.

"Where is the man that was here? What did he tell you?" he said and threatened.

That House on Dakota Street

I was suddenly filled with the right to protect my child and yelled back at him, "Get out of my house. Now!"

The man lowered the axe, released my son, and walked out of the house. He mumbled to himself words that I could not make out. I ran to the front door and locked it, and then I searched the rest of the house. It was all clear, but fear settled into us both.

"Mama, I'm scared," Casey said and clung to me after the search.

"I know, son," I said. I had had enough. I decided that I was going to use whatever power of attorney that I had, and I was going to take my son away first thing in the morning. To hell with this place, I thought.

6

That House on Dakota Street

I was not easily scared. I had been in the military, and I had faced a nasty divorce. I was a tough girl, except when it came to anything that I could not explain. The next morning, more nerve was required as the day started with Tommy. He was knocking on my back door and shouting.

"Jo! Jo! Wake up!" he yelled out. I greeted him a few minutes after that while wearing my nightgown. I was a confused lady with frizzled hair and a long yawn to match.

"What the hell do you want, Tommy!" I demanded.

"I came over to invite you to breakfast, but I found your garden all trampled over," he said.

"What?" I asked. I wrapped my coat tightly around me and tied my belt. I made sure that I was at least wearing my slippers. I was not fully awake yet.

After I walked down the steps, I looked from the edge of the patio on the left side of the carport and viewed the destruction. The corn was destroyed, and there were small holes all over the half-acre garden. Either there had been an invasion of groundhogs, or I had been visited again by the man and his axe.

"What happened?" I asked.

"I was going to ask you the same question," Tommy said.

I got dressed and gave Tommy some coffee, and I poured milk and cereal for Casey. Within the hour, an unmarked police car showed up at the carport. The old man had forced my hand, and Tommy had insisted on calling the authorities.

"Ma'am," the officer said, as he came into the kitchen. I asked Casey to go watch television, but he refused. He had seen the holes and wanted to be treated like an adult. Tommy disapproved of my liberal attitude, but I allowed him to stay.

Chapter 6

"It's ok, officer. We can talk in front of him," I said. "We both saw the guy last night. He just came inside—like it was nothing to him. He held up an axe at my son. The night before—he was at my window."

"Well, if nothing else, I have to take him in," the officer said. His name was Frank Reading. His wife was the town librarian, and he was one of the local detectives—in fact, he was the only local detective. He was in a brown suit, but *he* was not awake yet either. I invited him to stay for coffee, before he went to the Johnson place.

"Coffee can wait. He may decide to run away," Frank said. "I better go."

Frank turned and opened the back door only to find Mr. Johnson standing at the door waiting for him. It shook us for a moment, until we realized that the old man's demeanour had changed since last night. I stood and blocked the view of the man from my son, and then motioned Frank and Tommy outside.

"I don't want no trouble," the old man said, as he calmly laid down his weapon and stepped down the stairs and away from the back door. He turned around, and he waited for the officer in the carport. Tommy and I followed the officer to view the curious surrender. I had questions that would not stop in my brain.

"Frank, I want to ask him some questions," I said, as I stepped closer to him.

"I don't recommend it, ma'am," Frank said, but he stepped aside when my look said that I was going to do it anyway.

"Mr. Johnson?" I started. "Why did you dig up my garden? And how do you know Mr. Jennings?" I then informed Frank and Tommy about my visit to a pawn shop and my dinner with Mr. Jennings. They both looked confused, but they let me continue my questioning of the old man.

34

That House on Dakota Street

"I wanted to make sure that you did not take anything," the old man said. "Everything in that house is mine—damn it!" He seemed more sane than anyone else that I had met at that moment. "I wanted to make sure you did not find a way in. Mr. Jennings is a liar!"

Frank twirled his eyes and fingers in a way that seemed to shout out, "crazy."

"Mr. Johnson," Frank interrupted. "Why don't you explain to us what you are talking about. This ain't your property. You have no business over here."

The old man refused to say anything else. He seemed to sense that no one knew what he was talking about. Perhaps, he felt safer by saying nothing more, I thought.

Frank led the calm old man to his car. He cuffed him and helped him into the back seat. Then he told me that he would be back. Frank told me that he had further questions for me.

"I want you to take me to that pawn shop, Ms. Danning," he said. "I'll be back soon."

Tommy then asked me some questions. Casey was still inside eating cereal. I had closed the back door just in time to prevent him from seeing or interacting with the old man again. He did not deserve any more trauma.

"What is this about a pawn shop?" Tommy asked as we both paced the carport. "What pawn shop are you talking about?"

I told him that I had found some items. I lied and said it was some jewelry that my grandmother had given me. I told him that I had only wanted an estimate, and I told him where the store was.

"Behind the grocery store on Main Street?" Tommy asked. "There ain't no pawn shop there. That is a restaurant. A Chinese restaurant, I think."

Chapter 6

Tommy came inside for another cup of coffee, and then he left just as confused as when he had arrived. Once Frank returned, I was determined to find some answers to the riddles. The last few days and my grandmother's death were beginning to shake my stability. Too many unanswered questions were hard to ignore.

Frank drove to me to the pawn shop, and we got out of the car. I left Casey in charge of a locked house.

I looked at the sign on the door that advertised the Chinese restaurant and its deal of the day. I walked in and Frank followed me with a look that said, "I think that *she* is just as crazy as the old man."

I confronted the nice man at the counter.

"Where is Mr. Jennings?" I asked with a shaken voice. "What have you done with all of the stuff that was here?"

"You want special?" he asked. "We have no Jennings."

Frank grabbed me by the arm gently, asked the man to forgive the behavior, and then he escorted me out. He told me that he was taking me to see his wife.

We drove to the library, and Frank insisted that I come in and talk to his wife, Carolyn, the librarian.

Chapter 7

C arolyn scanned several newspapers as the screen was tilted to where everyone could see it. She had pulled up some old copies of a 1939 newspaper, at the request of her husband.

"Look for Jennings, I know that I have heard that name before," Frank said.

After a few minutes of searching, Carolyn nailed it. She had the mystery solved, or at least part of it.

"You owe me dinner, and a night out, Mr. Reading," she smirked. She pointed to the article about the prison break. Frank and I leaned in and read the article.

Prison officials confirmed that the notorious J.R. Jennings has escaped. The criminal that slaughtered twenty college girls while at Howard University is no longer in jail. Police have set up roadblocks and are confident that he will be caught soon.

"Oh, there's more," Carolyn grinned. The scanner switched to another view. This time it was the internet. It was a database with marriage records. "Frank, on a hunch, I looked up that old couple that used to live in the Johnson place. The couple purchased the property in 1908. They were George and Hazel Cunningham."

"So?" Frank said.

"Look," she said. "Hazel's maiden name on a marriage certificate in 1907 was Jennings."

Carolyn's grin indicated that there was more information.

"And?" Frank asked and smiled back.

"Johnson?" I interrupted.

"Correct," Carolyn said. "She was married before to a man named Johnson."

"So the courthouse claim to the property was legitimate," Frank said. "The family was simply moving into their relatives house. But was does Jennings have to do with any of this?"

That House on Dakota Street

"I don't know, Frank," Carolyn said. "*You're* the detective—not me."

"Frank, can you get me some men and a bulldozer?" I interrupted again. "I need to dig a hole in my grandmother's garden."

8

That House on Dakota Street

Casey was sitting on the back porch steps eating potato chips while I walked around in the carport. Frank and Tommy were at the edge of the garden watching the sight. The dirt was sitting in several piles around the middle of the garden and the men had switched to shovels.

Once they finally hit something, we were invited to the scene. They had found what appeared to be a piece of solid wood about six to twelve feet below the topsoil. Drills were brought in to dig through it.

While this was going on, the Johnson family, minus the jailed old man, was standing in their yard watching the event. They seemed just as curious as we were. Occasionally, Tony would cuss us all out with various words of profanity that only *he* could understand.

A ladder was brought in and placed down into the hole. I had to order Casey back because his curiosity had become so overwhelming. As for me, I insisted on going in with Frank and the others to view the contents. However, before we could start on the journey down the ladder, a truck pulled up beside the garden, and a tall man with long braided hair exited.

"Ms. Danning?" the man shouted to me. We stood and looked down the hole, but we waited for the man to approach. He was a man dressed in jeans and a Western shirt and cowboy boots. He was friendly and direct.

"May I come with you?" he asked.

"Henderson? What are *you* doing here?" Frank asked. It was revealed that Mr. Henderson was from one of the private colleges nearby. Carolyn had blabbed to her colleagues and word was getting out that something was happening at the Johnson place. Henderson was in charge of Native-American studies.

Chapter 8

"I *need* to be here, Frank," Mr. Henderson said. "I want to see what is inside. With your permission, ma'am," he asked me.

I agreed to the additional visitor, and then Casey came running up to the scene. I suspected that Casey had also eavesdropped when the old man had surrendered as well. It was one for all.

Frank followed two workers down the ladder, and then he motioned for everyone else to follow. The first flashlights were enough to light the place, but it was still somewhat dark. More flashlights followed and the place began to show itself.

"I'll be damned," Frank said. "It's a cemetery!"

Dozens of wooden coffins were stacked against the sides of the room. And toward the back, toward the direction of the Johnson family home, there were piles of gold bars. That must be the treasure that the old man was guarding, I thought. The old man had dug the holes in the garden thinking that he had a hole that needed to be patched. In his paranoid state of mind he had thought that I was after his gold. Perhaps the only Johnson to know about this was the old man, I thought.

The next discovery solved another mystery. It was a skeleton that was dressed in a prison uniform. He sat in a wooden chair, and it looked as if the skeleton was watching us. Beside him were two additional coffins. A door behind the sitting skeleton was locked, and again, it led in the direction of the Johnson place. The door was busted open and a foul smell permeated the air.

"Cool," Casey blurted out. "This is the best day ever!"

The next room had dozens of skeletons in the dirt without a coffin. At the end of the room, there was a set of stairs that obviously led up to the Johnson house.

Everyone was ordered out of the room, at the advice of the workers, as the air became difficult to breath. We all inhaled the fresh air with great satisfaction, once we were back on top of the ground.

"I suppose that Jennings came back and murdered his parents for some reason or another," Frank said to me as we climbed out. We brushed off all of the dirt from our clothes and sat on the grass near the back porch.

The hired workers excused themselves and left us. They spoke little English and were uncomfortable being around the hole of death. Tommy, Frank, and Mr. Henderson sat down with Casey and me on the lawn.

It was determined later that the man in the prison uniform was indeed J.R. Jennings, the escaped convict. He had come home and killed his parents and had died underground. Later the old man confessed to having locked the basement door and sending the man to his death. He brought the rest of his family to the house years later when he found out that the place was going to be sold. He did, in fact, forge the papers, but it was his mother that had been one of the victims. The other skeletons without coffins were dozens of the evicted Cherokee tribe that had been piled on top of each other. The remaining coffins were African Americans that did not make a successful escape out of the county during the running of an underground railroad to freedom. It was a graveyard of confusion, but it answered a lot of questions. The gold was from a prison. Historical records confirmed that a load of gold had been stolen in the late 1800's near the location. There were many unanswered questions, but the biggest question of all was the mysterious Mr. Jennings—the man that had only been seen by two people.

◆ ◆ ◆ ◆

Chapter 8

Casey told police that he had been watching television during his mother's visit with Mr. Jennings. He had not seen the stranger. I recalled that I had taken a plate of food into the living room for him because he did not wish to miss a documentary that was on. As for the old man, he died in jail shortly after the diggings. We never knew the complete story of how he had stumbled on the house as a child and had locked up the convict in a supposed moment of panic. Maybe he was nothing more than an unsung hero. He was asked later by investigators about Mr. Jennings, but he had forgotten about the whole incident. Some people say that he lost his entire mind, while others claimed that I was the only crazy person in the entire story.

9

The cool sea air was blowing on my face, while my body was protected from the sun by my large umbrella. Casey was playing in the water with some new friends, and I was falling asleep with a crime novel resting on my shirt. My naked toes were curled in the sand. I was just beginning to fall asleep—when I was suddenly interrupted.

"Ms. Danning?" the youthful voice repeated itself.

I leaned up from my towel and adjusted my sunglasses to view the man dressed in shorts and a T-shirt. He flashed a badge quickly at me and introduced himself.

"I'm agent Jackson," he said.

He didn't look like an agent, or any policeman either. I took off my sunglasses to get a complete view, and then I sat up. The sea breeze of Wilmington continued to pound us, and we were hit with several strong gusts. My umbrella blew over.

"Ok. You have my attention, Mr. Jackson," I told him.

I had been in Wilmington about three months, and I was getting used to the idea of no more mysterious men approaching me. The remaining Johnson family members were allowed to live in their house, and my grandmother's house and garden were transferred to a historical society. I had left Taylor behind with no regrets.

"Ms. Danning, I understand that you can talk to dead people?" he asked me.

I knew from that moment on that I would always have steady employment. I just did not realize that the road ahead would be so full of incredible adventures—stories that I could never even imagine.

That House on Dakota Street

We hoped that you enjoyed this short story. Please visit our website at Http://RaeTAlexander.com and feel free to leave a review at Http://www.Amazon.com.

www.ingramcontent.com/pod-product-compliance
Lightning Source LLC
Chambersburg PA
CBHW071220130626
46555CB00004B/1782